MY OWN STORY BOOK

belongs to:

....

I have read
up to here

MY OWN STORY BOOK

Judy Hindley

ILLUSTRATED BY
ROBERT BARTELT
AND
TONI GOFFE

KINGFISHER BOOKS

Kingfisher Books, Grisewood & Dempsey Ltd,
Elsley House, 24–30 Great Titchfield Street,
London W1P 7AD

First published in 1990 by Kingfisher Books

BRITISH LIBRARY CATALOGUING IN PUBLICATION DATA
Hindley, Judy
My own story book.
I. Title   II.Bartelt, Robert and Goffe, Toni
823'.914 (J)
ISBN 0 86272 519 4

Cover illustration by Toni Goffe
Cover design by Terry Woodley
Phototypeset by SPAN (Southern Positives and
Negatives), Lingfield, Surrey
Colour separations by Scantrans Pte Ltd, Singapore

Printed in Spain by Salingraf, S.A.L.

CONTENTS

Run along now

"Run along,"
said Mum.

"Run along,"
said Dad.

"Run along,"
said Grandpa.

"Run along,"
said Gran.

"Run along,"
said Albert.

"Run along!" said Gill.

So they ran . . .

. . . and ran . . .

. . . and ran . . .

7

. . . and ran . . .

. . . and ran . . .

. . . and ran . . .

. . . till everyone said
"Stand still!"

9

Little Brown Bird
finds a home

Little Brown Bird was ready
to lay some eggs.
But she had no home.
"Oh deary, deary me!"
said Little Brown Bird.
"Where can I find
a good home
for my eggs?"

She went to Dog.

"I'm ready
to lay my eggs,"
she said.
"But I have
no home.
Can we live
with you?"

"What a silly
you are!"
said Dog.
"I chase
little birds.
This is no home
for you.
You can take
some threads
from my blanket.
But
THAT IS ALL."

Little
Brown
Bird
flew off
and told
her husband.

Then she went to Horse.

"I'm ready
to lay my eggs,"
she said.
"But I have
no home.
Can we
live with you?"

"What a silly
you are!"
said Horse.
"I stamp at birds.
This is no home
for you.
You can take
some hay
from my box.
But
THAT IS ALL."

Little
Brown
Bird
flew off
and told her husband.

Then she went
to Cat
(but not too close).

"I'm ready
to lay my eggs,"
she said.
"But I have
no home.
Can we live
in your basket
when you're not
there?"

"What a silly
you are!"
said Cat.
"I *eat*
little birds.
This is no home
for you.
Take some fur
from my basket
IF YOU DARE."

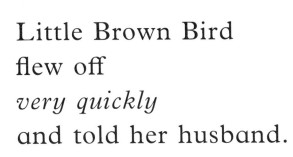

Little Brown Bird
flew off
very quickly
and told her husband.

She said,
"Dog won't
have us.
Horse won't
have us.
Cat will
eat us!
Oh, what shall
we do!"

"Ask Duck," said
her husband.

So Little Brown Bird
went to Duck.

"I'm ready
to lay my eggs,"
she said.
"But I have
no home.
Can we
live with you?"

15

"Of course!"
said Duck.
"You can live
in this nice mud
and swim with us."

"But we can't swim!"
said Little Brown Bird.

"Too bad!" said Duck.
"There is mud
and there is water
but
THAT IS ALL."

Little
Brown
Bird
flew off
and told
her husband.

"Perfect!" said
her husband.
"That is just
what we need."

Little
Brown
Bird
was very, very sad.

"I am ready
to lay
my eggs,"
she said.
"But I have
no home.
And I have
a crazy husband.
All we have
is mud, hay,
threads and fur.
What kind of home
is THAT!"

17

"Come and look!"
said her husband.

"Mud,

hay,

threads

and fur –

a perfect home
for little brown birds
like us."

And it was.

18

Four friends

Four friends
went
on a
fishing trip:

Monkey,   Hippo,   Lion

and Snake.

But their Mamas
called them back.

"Stop!"
called Mama Monkey,
as they
went
down
the path.

"Don't go!"
said Mama Hippo,
as they
began to run.

20

"Wait!"
said Mama Lion,
as they got on
the boat.

"Come back!"
said Mama Snake,

as the
boat
sailed
on . . .

21

"Why?" asked the friends.

"You forgot
your
lunch!"

So they all came back again.

The good and bad things about puppies

The good thing
about a puppy
is,
he likes to follow you.

The bad thing is,
he likes to follow you
everywhere.

The good thing is,
he likes
to sit
with you.

The bad thing is,
he likes
to sit
with you
in your chair.

The good thing is,
he can go
with you
to the dentist.

The bad thing is,
you have to take *him*
to the vet.

The good thing is,
he looks so happy
when you feed him.

The bad thing is,
he looks so sad
when you forget.

The good thing is,
he loves
to chase
a ball.

The bad thing is,
he hates
to give
it back.

The good thing is,
he likes to race
with you.

The bad thing is . . .

. . . he always wins.

The good thing is,
he licks your hands
to comfort you.

The bad thing is,
he tries
to lick your face
and neck,
and ears,
too.

"Shoo!"

Sometimes
when you call him,
he will *not*
come in.

And then
you have to call,
    and call,
    and look
    for him . . .

But when you find him,
you're so glad
to see him!

The best thing is,
a puppy is a friend.

Mr Wolf's dinner-time

A wolf
came to visit
some children.

He knocked
at the door.

KNOCK!
KNOCK!
KNOCK!

"Let me in,"
said
the wolf.

"I am
your
mother,
and
it's time
for
dinner!"

"Oh, no!"
cried the children.
"You are not
our mother.
We can hear
your sharp claws.
Go away!"

The wolf
went away,
and clipped off
his sharp claws.

Then
he went back.

KNOCK!
KNOCK!
KNOCK!

"Let me in,"
said the wolf.
"I am
your mother,
and it's time
for dinner!"

"Oh, no!"
cried the children.
"You are not
our mother.
We can see
your sharp teeth.
Go away!"

The wolf
went away,
and filed down
his sharp teeth.

Then
he went back.

KNOCK!
KNOCK!
KNOCK!

"Let me in,"
said the wolf.
"I am
your mother,
and I'm hungry!"

"Oh, no!"
cried the children.
"You are not
our mother.
We can see
your
wicked
eyes.
Go away!"

The wolf
went away,
and put on
dark glasses.

Then
he went back.

KNOCK!
KNOCK!
KNOCK!

"Let me in,"
said the wolf.
"I really am
your mother."

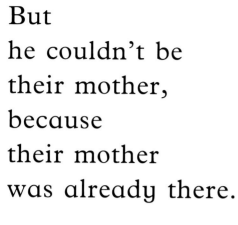

But
he couldn't be
their mother,
because
their mother
was already there.

"Oh, no!"
said the children.
"You couldn't be
our mother.
Besides,
we can still see
your
bushy
tail!"

The wolf
went away,
and shaved
his bushy tail.

As he went back,
everyone
laughed at him.

The wolf
was mad.

He was
so mad,
he ran
straight
at the door.

BUT –
this time,
the door
flew open.

"Come inside!"
cried the children.
"It's time
for dinner."

Poor
old
wolf!
He had no claws
to stop himself.
He had no teeth
to bite with.
He had no tail
to speak of
and
he could hardly see.

He went ZIP!

PLOP!

into the cooking pot.

And that night,
they had
Wolf Dinner.

And they had it
the next night

and

the next night

and

the next night . . .

until
they had all had
quite enough.

NO MORE WOLF!

— MENU —

SUNDAY —
ROAST WOLF

MONDAY —
COLD WOLF
AND SALAD

TUESDAY —
CURRIED WOLF

WEDNESDAY —
WOLF ON
TOAST

THURSDAY —
WOLFBURGERS
AND CHIPS

Bill, the perfect monster

All of Bill's family were monsters. They had green, greasy hair, and small, red eyes,

and they were perfectly horrible.

When Bill was born,
his Mum thought
he was perfect.

He yelled,
and howled,
and made
a terrible racket.

He threw things,
and broke things,
and made
a terrible mess.

As soon as
he got teeth,
he bit.

Soon he bit everything
that moved

and some things
that just stood there.

His family loved him.
They all said,
"Isn't he a perfect monster!"

But as Bill grew up,
he changed.
Little by little,
he got nicer.
One day,
when the family
was out,
Bill smiled.
"No, dear,"
said his Mum.
"Monsters
NEVER do that."

The next day,
he picked up
some litter
and put it
in the bin.

"Stop that!"
said his Dad.
"Monsters
NEVER
do that!"

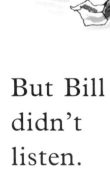

But Bill
didn't
listen.

Very soon,
he had all
the wrong
habits
for a monster.
He began to wash
his horrible face.

He began to comb
his horrible hair.

He even tidied
his horrible,
little bed
when no one
was looking.

When Monstrous Aunt
came to visit,
she was
most upset.

"What's wrong?"
she asked Bill's Mum.
"Your house
used to be
a *perfect mess*."

"Isn't it awful?"
said Bill's Mum.
"We come home
from a long,
hard night
of being monsters –
and there is Bill . . .

. . . cleaning the house
again."

"Send him out
to play!"
said Monstrous Aunt.

So they did,
but it was no use.

He didn't play
like the other
monster children.

"Send him to school!"
said Monstrous Aunt.
So they did,
but it was no use.

It was a very good school
for monsters.
The teacher tried
to teach Bill.
He showed Bill
how to scowl . . .

and growl,   and howl,

and yell perfectly   But Bill sang
horrible yells.   a sweet little song.

Then he showed Bill
how to grind
your teeth,

and tear things up

and bash
things down.

But Bill read
a nice little story.

Bill completely spoiled
the school photograph.

He was sent home
for teaching
the others
to take baths
and go to bed
when it was dark.

"Don't worry,"
said Bill's Mum
to his Dad.
"Perhaps he'll get
a really horrible job
like making earthquakes."

But Bill became
a cook.

"Never mind,"
said Bill's Dad
to his Mum.
"Perhaps he'll marry
a really horrible
monster girl."

But Bill married
a lovely monster girl
who was just like him.

They both got jobs
on a boat,
and sailed away.

Time went by.
Bill's Mum and Dad
got old.
They couldn't be
so monstrous
any more.

And they missed Bill.

At last, one day,
they got a postcard.
It was from Bill.

He was coming home
again!

When the day came
for Bill to come home,
they were so excited.

When the doorbell rang,
they hobbled to the door
as fast as they could.

There was Bill –
just as nice
as ever.

There was Bill's wife –
just as nice
as ever.

But behind them, there were . . .

. . . three horrible children.

"Look what we've got!"
cried Bill.
"THREE
PERFECT
MONSTERS!"

Bill's Mum and Dad
were perfectly happy
at last.

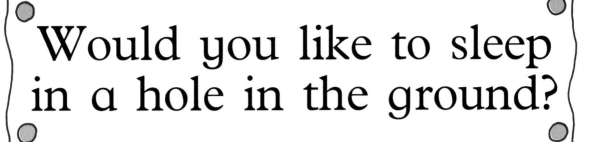

Would you like to sleep in a hole in the ground?

Would you like
to sleep
in a hole
in the ground?

Would you like
to sleep
in a tree?

Would you like
to snooze
in the ooze
of a pond –

or snore
in a bunch
like a bee?

Would you like
to sleep
on the wing
like a swift?

Would you like
to sleep
on the hoof?

Would you like
to hang
from your toes
all night –
upside-down
in the roof?

Would you like
to doze
in a dustbin?

Would you like
to curl up
in a cave?

Would you like
to dream
like a fish
in a stream –

or roll about
in a wave?

Would you like
to slumber
in rotten lumber
like a beaver
in a dam?

Or
are you happy
to jump into bed
at night,

snuggle up
tight,

turn out
the light

and imagine
whatever you like?

I AM!